# SW10

I0530586

South West x 10

By

**John F King**

York Europe Publishing 2017

ISBN  978-0-9931306-4-9

SW10 by **John F King**

**Contents-**

**www.johnkinginternational.eu**

# Binoculiar

What was it? The binoculars were top line, there was no fault in the way of seeing, it was what. Dolphin? Even that most charming of creatures does not stay still for that long. Seal. Same difference. Gull. I could tell that with the naked eye. Could there be an explanation that I didn't know I could know about? Everyone says these are strange times. No specifics. 'These are strange times', local people say to undercurrents of universal agreement with no care to define what times, what strangeness.

There was no doubt there was something there, on the rocks, below the castle.

There was, by any recent measure, no doubt these were strange times. On that other Atlantic coast, unexpected outcomes, politics, climate, making waves on our side. The Baner Peran flew again over the old fort, nationalism on every shore.

In former times a chain was stretched across the harbour, raised to prevent access by cross channel foes. Who imagined such measures could rise again?

I resumed speculation, elimination. Fact – there was definitely a shape in the water, the above marine life was ruled out, what did that leave? Inanimate object? Driftwood, plastic, clay, all impossible.

I alternated between naked eye and the magnification. I needed to think in a new way, a way more in tide with the times, an unidentified floating object, military? Strange smoking ships had been visible on the horizon on route to wars we saw on television screens. But here, in our harbour?

It was then I saw it – it was looking at me. A periscope, a hideous wink, what was below the surface, a defector from the Clyde, Balaklava, the Potomac, the Tamar? If only it was a *pyffyer*, the watcher of the waters.

What mystery is the sea, whose stirrings speak of a hidden soul beneath.

~Melville

# Breaking Point

Everyone thought they were a couple except them. Not in the conventional sense, but what is conventional? Starting each other's sentences, drinking from the same glass, getting changed in the van without a screen, perhaps they were a kind of couple. Nothing odd about it.

The band were upfront about their non-originality. Stones and Clash covers, inevitable Beach Boys. In the break between the sets Sal picked up K's glass, crowd surfed to the bar and returned with two Korevs.

A girl with a blurred transfer tattoo was with K when Sal returned.

'Surfers Against Sewage' the girl said to K ' so you do believe in something' and was re-engulfed by the crowd.

K lifted his glass to Sal– 'To the wave, man'

Sal clinked back, 'cheers, K.'

The band played an encore without being asked, a geographically modified version of *Surfin' USA*.

'One for the road? ' said K

'Yeah, one and gone' said Sal, 'early start.'

The road was the Atlantic Highway, home, a 12 year old VW California was parked on it.

5.59 AM Sal used her t shirt as an internal windscreen to clear the overnight condensation.

6 AM she ran her hand over K's second skin. K slept in a wet suit, why waste time when there are waves to catch?

' Morning K,' said Sal.

'Is it a good one?' asked K

They exchanged a smile as they parked up outside Hayle, the sky so grey and low they felt high.

'You think today is the day?' asked Sal.

'I always think that, man, ' said K, ' I always will. Question is does He think so.'

Sal continued smiling, there is no reason why the surfing God shouldn't be a man. If K wanted to think that no harm in it.

K had driven the California the length of the North Coast, looking for the big one, today was always the day even when it wasn't. Sal, born in Bradford, never learned to drive, and was 18 before she first saw the sea. She bombed her MPhil in Falmouth on her second day, committed only to the lifelong learning of surfing.

People off the coast talked of K, no one knew where he was from. His present was like a wave, no past, probably no future, nothing ever repeated the same way, a short present.

If you looked at the black row of specks in the surf K was always the one out of line, further out, pushing to breaking point, searching for the Bombura, a search that could never be fulfilled.

At the end of each day they repaired to the California. In the van Sal talked, K listened. He wasn't quiet, just didn't talk much. Sal was cool with that. People who talked a lot never had anything to say, words can really sink you.

Nights were never late, mornings always early. Midsummer you could snooze on the shore, nights barely existed. This time of year most had gone back to the big inland cities from which they, like Sal, had evolved. Sal never went back now, wouldn't even want to live in a house. K once said what is the point of bricks, they don't float.

Off grid, off shore, barely visible from land, K went further and further out, the endless quest. Even Sal had third thoughts but kept them to herself. Where could this end, could it end well, a quest for a wave, is that asking for peace or asking for trouble?

One evening on a rare fourth Korev – Beer and salt water don't mix – she asked K if he had any regrets.

K looked back at her for ages before saying 'what do you mean , man?'

'Regrets, looking back, doing things differently, something you did or said years ago that hurt someone.'

'I never said anything,' said K. ' I never hurt anyone.'

Sal said ' do you want to ask me if I have any regrets?'

K said, ' does the sea have any regrets?'

Sal rode it out. She wondered why she even asked and smiled. Portishead seeped through the van sound rig working with the silence.

She looked at K, he seemed about to say something.

He said 'early start' and zipped up the wet suit.

The next dawn he was gone before she was encased in her suit. She searched every wave but they broke without him.

# Festival

-Do something

-I don't think it is my place to

-Do something

You could feel the crowd coming alive. In the wrong way. They weren't, at least so far,  the sort of people who would engage in slow hand clapping or violence but anything can go that way if people are pushed.

-Do something, she said again. For the director of the most prestigious literary festival in the south west I was more concerned at her lack of vocabulary than the late running of the key note speaker.

-You're a writer, said the director accusingly, you understand these people, why is she late? If this is some kind of artistic statement I'm not impressed.

-I have no more insight into why she is late than you do.

In my mind I ran through the possibilities of why Beth Tregowan could be late. True it was my idea to book her. A US writer with a local sounding name, would people realise the journey involved? Maine to Manhattan, JFK to whichever runway on Heathrow they allocated to writers, the so-called Great Western to St Erth, what could possible go wrong. I wanted her perspective on the US elections, an insight into her writing techniques, the literary equivalent of trickle-down theory. My own work had indeed been compared to her middle period. I took this as a compliment.

-This is unprofessional, said the director. I wouldn't tolerate this from a bus conductor, an electrician, why should we tolerate this from a …

-Writer? I said.

-Your word not mine, she said. You call yourself a writer. I want you to get up there and entertain them.

-I said I'm a writer not an entertainer

-Do it

-They haven't come to see, hear me

-True. But they are not going to have come for nothing. And there will be no refunds. Understand?

The director outstared me. I felt my legs climb the stairs to the stage and walk to the rostrum. I laid my notebook on the stand and looked out. I heard my voice say – Ladies and gentlemen, due to circumstances beyond our control Beth Tregowan has been unavoidably detained.

There was a silence in the hall. What did I expect, a mass walk out? No one moved. I gripped the lectern.

It was I who broke the silence. I'd always said to myself I would never use the word 'However' but if there was ever a moment this was it.

-However, I said, with your permission I would like to read to you from my own collection of short stories *The Land Beyond the Coast*.

I never waited for the permission. Rhetorical questions are cheap, I know.

I broke the silence again. I began to read. At the end of my first story I looked out again into the hall. The silence continued but it had changed in tone. It seemed to give me permission to start another one. How much was value for money? More. Less? The silence after the third story changed again. You could hear a pin drop. No clichés. I began a third. The silence grew warmer, it was only broken by a crash mid-way through my fourth story. I looked out into the hall.

The director had taken Beth Tregowan's suitcase as they banged through the double doors.

The crowd as one turned and uttered a unison 'shhhhhhhhhhhhh. In other circumstances, I would have called the crowd a mob.

The director without hesitation had walked up the steps and taken the lectern.

-Ladies and gentlemen, I do apologise for the delay and the imposition. I thank you for your forbearance, without further delay, please welcome to our festival the famous writer Beth Tregowan.

She began to clap but it didn't take. After three solo claps she was forced to stop. It was a standoff. A write off. Me, the director, Beth Tregowan, the crowd.

A voice floated through the hall , mid row, left back perhaps, a lady in a hat. She had the presence to look directly at me from that distance.

- I have forgotten your name, dear, or perhaps you forgot to introduce yourself. We don't want the famous writer, we want you, you may not be a famous writer now. You will when you finish your story.

# Goonhilly

Everything is comparative.

Richmond to Helston. 300 miles, a night as black as deep space. At least the journey wasn't infinite.

I'd logged the call at 2247 the previous evening. I wasn't asleep, I wasn't awake, I wasn't expecting anything to happen.

I'd often wondered what the call would be like if it ever came. I mean did we want the call, welcome it or fear it?

The Earth Station had been on stream since 1962. There had been a few interesting calls since then, generally on the morning of April 1 or some Steedy duty officer binge watching *Quatermass* pressing the wrong button at 4AM.

The ministry phone rang in my study downstairs.

'I don't want to disturb the minister, I thought I'd disturb you first. Not interrupting anything am I?'

The undersecretary had made various attempts to crack my private life. I merely wanted to make sure I had one.

'Not at all,' I filled, 'what's up?'

'Not exactly sure. The Goonhilly chaps have picked something up. I've already checked out it needs checking out. I want you to go down and ascertain how real this one is. For real.'

'Now?'

'You said I wasn't interrupting anything. At least Richmond is on the right side of town for the South West. I could ring your number two but I know she's in St John's Wood this evening. Probably a couple of drinks down too by this hour I shouldn't wonder.'

My non-drinking had always been a problem in the office.

It seemed small minded to demur. If the Goonhilly chaps had at last picked something up 300 million miles away it wouldn't be well received to make comparisons.

I flicked around on the Alfa Romeo media screen. Holst gave way to Pink Floyd, a 3AM DJ thinking no one of any discernment was still listening. No news flashes of note.

On arrival I was mildly surprised to be offered a cafetiere rather than the usual plastic. The director appeared before the first cup was cool enough to drink.

'Kuiper,' she said.

'Good morning director, I replied, 'Actually it's Stern.'

She regarded me for an instant, the line between humour and insubordination is virtually undetectable at this hour.

'Good morning, Stern,' she managed. No Mr. Pleasantries over it was black to science.

'Kuiper belt, mid to earth side, not exactly sure yet, but I, we have never known anything like it. Do you want to listen in?'

There was still a trace of burr in her accent, no one was sure if she had acquired it or hadn't totally lost it. Credibility was everything in this line of work.

She held the Bose phones out to me. I wasn't sure what to expect. 300 million miles away, closing in on the West Country, I mean what kind of accent would they have?

My ears were still adjusting from the late-night DJ above the hum of the Alfa cruising on the M4. The phones emitted a steady stream of a mid-tone signal, a Oldfield-esque B flat hum.

The director and I look at each other. The real thing?

'It's still too far out to be sure, We've booked you into The Old Temperance House, the Premier Inn was full. Take a break, snooze off the tinnitus, come back later this afternoon, we'll have a better fix then, work it out over dinner.'

We'd waited over two millennia, what difference does a day make?

The bed in the Old Temperance House afforded me about two hours sleep, I took a turn on the coastal path, the Mediterranean style waters clearing my head.

In the time I'd walked 2 miles, they, the as yet unspecified they had travelled two million miles. If they were coming, it would be tomorrow.

In the Goonhilly canteen the director ordered the dish of the day. She had three assistants with her. They were introduced but their names and titles went over my head, What they said didn't.

The director introduced the first assistant.

'This is Hill,' again no Mrs, Miss, Ms, Dr. 'Hill is operations leader, Deep Space Communications.'

Hill wore a Chanel type jacket with pens in a top pocket but there was nothing mixed about her signals. 'We are virtually certain we have detected a signal from an unspecified life force. It is data only, no language, as to be expected, but the current trajectory is earth, we should have a visual this evening, ETA 7.47.

Hill expounded: 'of course it is not the primary function of this Earth Station to actively or passively search for life forms other than our own. That would be a by-product of our other work. The assumption that all life forms are dependent on water and air as we define it is exactly that, an assumption. We are not in the business of theology or pseudo science. But his signal is strong, becoming stronger.. There is no other explanation. Whatever we may think ourselves about our depleted planet in terms of natural resources it is, one might more than speculate a des-res, a desirable residence in any known comparison to what is out there.'

She made a shooting star type wave up at the night sky. We were now lined up outside the station in a kind of solar system ranking order of our own, the director at the centre like the sun, hill her moon, myself in near orbit representing the ministry, the other assistants in rings beyond.

I was on a live feed to the minister in London. The director glared at me. 'switch that off, I've declared a Radio Quiet Zone, this is more than a once in a lifetime event, I don't want any interference. From anyone, anything.'

Away from street lights, away from everything the night was brilliant. I had never seen anything like it or heard such a silence. It was one of the assistants in our outer ring the broke it. 'There,' he said, ' west, closing.'

There could be no mistake, not a star, a satellite, a joker with a laser, a lost hang glider. How can you describe something no-one has ever seen before?

The object came closer and closer, then as suddenly as it appeared it regained altitude and moved higher and on, onto another trajectory.

Silently we returned to the monitors inside. The object had flown past us and was heading into God knows what beyond.

It was the first time I had ever seen the director at a loss. 'Why,' she said, ' why would they do that?'

Hill crashed the stillness. 'Why assume we have anything they could want?'

# Knight Trane

*'-You find no man, at all intellectual who is willing to leave London.'*

Arthur replayed the Johnson quote like an internal tannoy as the GWR left Paddington. There was no one to see him depart. Arthur had fallen from off scene, off screen. Going west was to him now a one channel selection.

'It's such a long way from anywhere,' people had said to him whenever he said, 'I'm thinking of a change of scene. London perhaps.' This was long before he coached himself out of beginning sentences ' I'm thinking of...' Best thing is to send postcards when you've arrived.

It was quotes, or more accurately clichés spoken audibly to Arthur that had moved him to leave the west in the first place. Not to his face of course, it wouldn't be in anyone's self-interest to say to the head of news, big fish small pond or some other suitable oceanic expression, preferably more original. But this was *Spotlight South West*, the premier news show in the South West, as Jon Snow said at the awards dinner. When Arthur accepted the RTS award for newsroom of the year he made the joke interspersing the words 'best' and 'only'.

When Arthur had disembarked the Night Riviera arriving at Paddington that early morning years or was it months earlier it was a different story. Arthur walked on water. The Plymouth newsroom was, truth be told, pleased to see the back of him. Who wants a regional prima donna who never makes a move?

The corner-less newsroom of Broadcasting House suited Arthur perfectly. He hadn't come here to hide.

'We'll start you on the 6pm' said Sidiq, 'We can move you earlier into the day or later into the night depending on the feedback.'

Not many headlines later Arthur settled into the 10pm seat. Most nights after delivering the sign off line ' now it is time for the news where you are' he repaired to Dean Street. Timing is everything.

It was so late at night that *Breakfast* TV was on in Sid's office that morning when Arthur judged the time was right for make a bigger pitch.

'Working title *Arthur's Round Table*,' Arthur launched straight into it.

'Been done before,' said Sid

Arthur segued on ' regional, national, international guests. Politics, cuisine, culture, sport, a world without boundaries, subjects without limits…

'Everything is nothing.' said Sid, 'stick to the autocue. Trust me.'

Sidiq was old school. An alumni of *Look North* he had nothing against regional types who moved to London, he had against news readers who invariably came to him after15 months wanting to become news makers. If they did it was usually for all the wrong reasons.

'Look, here is the guest list for the first show.'

'Make sure you have a show before you invite people on to it, Arth, basic show biz lore. Trust Me.

'Look.' He thrust the paper at Sid.

Sid read from the napkin 'Dean Street Soho House. You been home at all since 10.31 last night, Arth?'

'Other side,' said Arthur.

He sat back as Sidiq read the fantasy guest list: a surfer who was making waves in a boy band, a baker who was reputed to now supply the Lanesborough, an actress turned children's laureate who had invested in a wind farm near Newlyn and subsequently in a farm converted to look like a lighthouse near Talland.

'So. I'm glad you're not lonely,' said Sid

'I see where you are coming from,'

'I don't think you can,' said Sid ' but I can see where you are.'

Sid stared him out, then moved his stare to the door. Producers were the only people in the newsroom to have offices, at least Sidiq was. Arthur walked through it. 'I'll review the guest list,' was his Parthian shot.

'In my experience guests aren't the problem in chat shows,' said Sid.

It was then that Sid made an unusual move. He raised himself from his Eames and put his arm round Arthur in the open area.

'I don't do advice,' said Sid, 'you arrived at Paddington, me at Kings Cross, if you make it that non-intern way you can do it your way.'

'But..' said Arthur.

'But,' said Sidiq, 'when you're Off Air at 1030pm a glass of Montrachet at the Garrick may be de rigeur. I mean a glass, I mean the Garrick, I mean well. Get me?'

The list delivered over *Breakfast* the next day was a marginal improvement. A chef who graduated from the Box Tree, by-passed London to proceed directly to personnel director at Jamie's 15, a Turner prize winner who was paid to paint graffiti into a defined space at the Tate St Ives, an American Airlines flight engineer who had requested political asylum after diverting to Newquay International.

'An improvement, granted,' said Sid, noting the reverse Garrick logo, 'but…'

'But…'

'The list isn't the issue.'

'But..'

'Go home,' said Sid. He'd read in the Evening Standard's *Londoner*'s *Diary* of the newsreader who had bought a new pad in Battersea but was rarely seen there, ' put some curtains up.'

Sid looked at the logo on the third list Arthur proffered while rather loudly saying something about the biggest on screen moment since that film scene where de Niro meets Pacino.

He didn't even turn the paper over. Arthur protested. Sid made a sweeping movement with his right arm while opening a desk drawer with the left. 'Let me read you something,' said Sid.

The drawer was full of envelopes, some printed, some handwritten. Sidiq took one at random and took out the letter from the already slit top-

'I forgave Bosanquet his minor slips, anyone can become tired, but Knight is in a different category and a different era. I do not pay my licence fee, and hence your salary - for this.'

Sid produced another –

'It would seem unfair to blame the autocue loader, I doubt it is his or her belief that Lituania is the flash point of the Balkan Crisis or the Single Market will be replaced by a Fair-Trade Festival.'

Arthur interjected ' what about the list, Sid?'

'I prefer Sidiq. What about these letters, emails, tweets? The list goes on' Sidiq made a sweeping gesture with his left hand to indicate the missives were more or less limitless, and held up a paper with a BBC header in his right hand.

'Some research for you, Arthur. Time sensitive. Tip. Take it from me.'

Arthur automatically read the print out aloud-

London Paddington depart 9.06 arrive Penzance 1439.

'It's first class' said Sidiq

'It's a single,' said Arthur.

# North by South West

The day was floating to a new sunset. Another day on the perfect holiday. The only cloud above each day passed meant there was one less to go. Not that I had a problem with going home. But we were speculating on how someone else's day would end.

'He's not Jesus, he's just a fella,' you said. At first I thought it was another of your film quotes, easier than some. But that wasn't the answer.

After so long by the sea we had decided to be on it. It was the right choice, even the tide was with us. We joined the herons in the higher reaches of the estuary, looked at the castle at lower reaches where the water doesn't know if it is sea or river.

The driver – is that the right word? We live so far inland - of the boat was affable. We speculated about his appearance and demeanour. Late-period Lennon spectacles, the white mini beard, the sawn-off denims. The keyboard player in a long forgotten prog band never asked to reform, an SBS officer (ret'd) with transferable skills, a victim or perpetrator of a banking crash who saw it all coming and bonused into a motor launch?

He improvised his commentary in an estuarine accent. Did it vary with the tide? It was interesting for us, how interesting must it be for him by the fifth time of each day? It was informative enough, the local knowledge tempered with an awareness of the wider world as we cruised past loading cargo boats bound, he said, for Gothenburg, Helsinki. Perhaps the world was flat beyond that.

The tour was good value, we estimated he made a reasonable living from it, perhaps not enough for the homes on top of the hill but certainly half way. He took the money from us and our sailing companions and cast off. First we turned left – was that east – past the sandbanks, beyond the inner harbour buoys. Gulls followed us, attracted by the wash of the propeller or lulled by his commentary. We turned seawards, looking back across the bay we could see our hotel. We had made the right choice.

The tour ended where it began, quayside, we disembarked for tea. The driver had tea from his flask as he reloaded his boat with more customers. We watched him cast off again. As we resumed our land tour of the harbour town, the galleries, the tea rooms. In the afternoon sun I bought Christmas cards at the RNLI shop – it seemed in every one's interest. At regular intervals we heard his boat chug back, disembark, reload, cast off until his day too ended.

Intrigued we watched his close of day routine. He drove the empty boat back to the inner harbour and tied up. On his own he went through his terminal manoeuvres, checking the engine, the moorings, tucking the boat in with a tarpaulin. That is when the speculation started. How would he get back? Yards out to sea, no auxiliary dinghy. Helicopter, submarine, seduce a mermaid? It concerned us more than him.

We continued to watch from dry land. You thought my suggestion that he could walk on water flippant. There are many men with white beards, they aren't all Jesus. I wasn't so sure, there was something about him, something you couldn't place. Do you need to put him in a box, you said.

I looked at you, distracted from the speculation. It was a holiday after all. I didn't want any clouds.

'He's not Jesus, he's just a fella,' you said finally. I looked at you again. When I looked back at the boat it was empty, alone with a buoy for the night. I looked back at you. He nodded to us as he walked past then away up the hill. A heron caught the last ray of the sun.

# Revert

As catastrophes go it wasn't that bad. Perhaps there was still some time left. The point was there was no way of knowing, in advance, how long. A month, a decade. This area of the island had been in bad shape for a while. People laughed at me when I first discussed it, kill joy was one of the more printable comments.

I don't know when it first started. People used to come here for holidays. Almost all by road, petrol, diesel, the hybrids never progressed, the electrics never really took hold. When the sea took the rail the airports reopened, only made things worse though statistics were produced to prove everything was much better.

More and more people came. Fewer left. Derelict homes were bought up , mines were converted. Even people who came in tents or motorised vehicles you could live in stayed. Why go back, this was the place to be, this land of sea and natural beauty. That was the paradox, the more people who were attracted by the natural beauty the less beautiful it became. It was unsustainable. One day- who knows when -we'd all fall off a cliff.

The roads in became dual carriage way, then three lane, then four. When the traffic became so one way the authorities simply closed the eastbound lanes, doubling the lane capacity in one move.

At first people liked it, seasons without rain, Christmas on the beach, the perma-attire of shorts and flip flops. Who wouldn't. Manufacturers of woollen goods, suppliers of logs failed or adapted to the new but power hungry industries- aircon, desalination. Wind farms became fans.

There was change in the air. Still I was laughed at but the denials became so insistent they must have known I had a point. A few of us decided we needed to do something now, do it ourselves, some people would rather die than be laughed at. Not me.

Now was the time for action. Non-violent of course. Inclusive, all who believed could join us. We cycled to the main gates of the complex expecting to be met by security. The gate house was in darkness. Inside we saw one security guard, his white asthmatic face illuminated by a mobile phone screen. He put down the phone, evidently all alone.

'I'm the only one left,' he coughed.

'Join us if you want,' I heard myself say without hesitation.

He passed me two keys, one for each dome he explained. Strangely it had never occurred to me they would be locked, an answer to a question I hadn't asked.

'Tropical or Mediterranean?' he asked.

'I'll take both,' I said.

The biodomes of the leisure complex had long been academic. The plants that originally could only flourish inside them were now everywhere, visitors had become confused and eventually stopped coming. The domes were totally intact but curiously inverted, exotic on the outside. Inside one there were oaks, ash, roses, in another fir trees, berries.

We locked ourselves in and made ourselves at home. I wished I had brought a coat but I stopped complaining.

# Subsidiarity

Berlin still had the wall when I first came here. Places change, people change, people change places, places change people. I knew St Ives was living in the past even then, but a Berliner isn't going make a big deal about that. I remember the exchange as a time of positive impressions, when the Schiffbauerdamm came to the Minack, Nina Hagen was rumoured to support The Pretenders at Truro, a Liebermann installation in the Hepworth garden.

Now my own show had transferred from Steglitz-Zehlendorf to the Tate. When the crates were being loaded into the removal van I decided I wasn't going to go back. I told the gallery director, Malcolm. Everyone called him X. I wondered if I had a nickname too? I know how you British – should I say English or Cornish? – like your Spitznamen. I do prefer it to the Herr Doktor Professor styling at home. Home ? So you went back when there was a wall and you aren't going back when there is no wall, the director commented. But you won't be the first who came here for a change of scene and stayed.

It was two seasons before I could find any balance, the heavy rains before the spring, the summer crowds before the leaves fell into the sea. I commuted at first, from my winter let in Carbis Bay to the studio collective above Porthmeor.

The only commodity plentiful in St Ives was water, the sea, the rain. Money, for me, wasn't. I portfolioed together some teaching, online work, a couple of sales placed through the collective.

Socially too I struggled through the cliques, the jazz club, the tennis club, film club, the Labour club. I researched the Labour party , as I was told to call it , was the equivalent of the SPD but it only seemed to be concerned with its own procedures and observably ideologically and geographically weak. When they heard I was an artist, one man with a Stalin moustache and Lenin cap asked me to design some leaflets for the Labour campaign on the EU referendum, but I couldn't work out what the line was even when it was explained to me and no money was allocated.

Back in Carbis Bay one afternoon with no jazz, tennis, or Labour Party meeting there was a strange sound in the flat. By the time I had figured out it was the phone ring tone it had gone to voicemail.

'Samuel, X here, something might interest you, look might sound better in person, see you in The Sloop about 8?'

The evenings were getting light then, I walked along the coastal path, past the lifeboat station to The Sloop. The director, as I continued to call him, bought me a cider without asking me what I wanted.

As the small talk went on I tried to decipher if any of the topics he touched on were what he actually wanted to talk about before he eventually said ' town -twinning.'

'South West England, South West Berlin. We need to be a happening place. The councillors asked me to recommend a now artist for a town twinning installation. I thought of you.'

There would be an operating grant through the European Commission Education Audiovisual and Culture Executive Agency, expenses from the councils, studio time, recognition. I didn't need to think about it.

My proposal, a wave built of tin by the regenerated old pilchard landing area was accepted. I began sketching on receipt of my first instalment, casting on the second. It felt right to have this mission, to lose myself in work, in meaning.

One evening the director rang me from the pub. His voice seemed subdued, speaking over what sounded like a background of men singing a sailor's song. I said I was working but he insisted I come down.

I didn't like the atmosphere in the pub, more and more men arrived, none of them appeared to be sailors the songs, shanties they called them, grew louder and flatter, although I would hardly describe them as Mendelssohn to start with. There were fewer references to the sea, more to football.

'You realise what this means, Samuel, don't you?'

'What?' I said

'The news', he said in a shouted whisper. 'Don't you ever stop working?'

The UK was to leave the EU, so-called direct democracy, the funding for my project was to be withdrawn immediately, symbolic.

I walked home, the sea on one side, the railway on the other. Nothing had changed, everything had changed. I resolved to carry on. You can turn back tides with intention.

Not many nights later I cycled to Godrevy to meet X and a few Party dissidents, a reverse band of smugglers, exiles. A blue flag had been burned outside the pub, a black one hoisted. We could do it ourselves.

I mikveh'd the sculpture my way with Weisse beer and sang as many lines from Schiller as I could remember as my sculpture was unveiled, guerrilla style.

It was late next day when I cycled back to the site. The sculpture twisted, on one side the word 'telogyon', on the other the word 'foreigner' was spray painted.

It could have been better, it could have been worse.

# The Last Laugh

I always thought I knew when it would be time to stop. When the time came I wasn't too sure.

Awards aren't everything – you need to laugh at them – but they do open doors. Runner up, Perrier or Eddies as they are now.

Comedy store, radio 4 6.30pm slot, Channel 4 pilot amber lit. All the time I polished my gigs at the Apollo. Keep it short, keep it simple, leave 'em wanting more.

The joke was me, stories, improvs, how I borrowed more and more money in various ways to pay off deeper debt. Student loan to pay day banks to call centre shifts. I made up my own call centre script, an off off script where I told my life story to whoever would listen for the allotted 4 minute slot and asked them to contribute what they wanted.

The joke was on no one. Except perhaps Channel 4. Their loss was BBCs gain, the show  - *Pay Back Time* went out first on BBC3, but went viral. Of course the paradox is that after Amazon Prime bought it I was, bluntly, rich doing a show about debt. Looking back I knew it would catch up with me one day, but as long as that day was as faraway as a 25% loan who cares.

I called the house in Polruan Sunny Side. Having to make the last ferry home kept my drinking under control until I bought my own Crabber. TV rights aren't everything. My agent texted me incessantly asking me if I had new ideas, or at least a new concept.

I lost the contract on my phone along with everything else. It wasn't very funny.

There was a sharp knock on the door. I owed a lot of people money, agents, dealers, satellite dish installers. Staying in bed wasn't a bad option. The noise continued.

I quarter-opened the door. It was the woman opposite. She had a north London accent and had given me a piece of advice on my first day here. 'We out of towners need to make a tiny bit more effort to show we belong. Call over if there is anything I can help you with. I've been here 19 years now.'

I hate people who say 'a tiny bit', how could someone like that help someone like me.

I mumbled something even I couldn't catch and began to close the door.

'Are you alright?' she said, 'we haven't seen you for a long time.' Her accent had neutralised. My timing wasn't on enough to close the door before she saw through me into the kitchen. 'Look can you hang on for a second?'

Hang on? For what, for who, is this some kind of joke? She returned 4 minutes later with two packages. 'Bread, still warm, 'she said, 'elderflower juice freshly pressed. It'll be a nice change for you. From the Cognac.'

'How do you know?' I said, thinking she must be another prier until I remembered that the only thing I stayed meticulous about was the recycling.

'Look it's none of my business but didn't you used to be…I'm sorry the name eludes me.'

'I still am,' I said. ' whoever I used to be.' Except I wasn't, only the name was the same, and I was being rude.

I held out my hand, 'Bernie,' I said.

Gradually I drank more elderflower juice than stuff derived from grapes.

Many loaves later Enid said to me, 'the local pub is having an open mic night. Stand up, mainly, well people doing stand up until some fall over.'

'That's so bad its good' I said to Enid, big of me.

'It's how you started isn't it? It's a way back for you, should be a cinch with your experience. We'd be honoured if you came down. No, I mean really.'

'No. Thanks. Not what I do anymore.'

'What do you do, Bernard?' said Enid. I thought her departure, gripping the elderflower bottle rather abrupt.

At night it dawned on me what I was missing. Enid was right, should be a cinch, someone like me.

We walked to The Lugger together. I can't remember the last time I was in a pub. Enid put my name down for a slot. I thought when they saw my name I might get bumped up to a feature but nothing happened. I hadn't rehearsed anything, why would I with my experience, my material?

I heard my name over the PA and moved to the dais. As I stood there a brilliant light shone in my face. All I had to do was improvise. Cinch.

Looking back I realise they were quite charitable really. I knew I'd died and there was no heaven. It seemed an eternity before any regulars broke the silence. 'In your own time, chief,' or 'say something or we'll laugh.'

The next thing I heard myself say was to the barman, was it the same night?

'Double brandy  no ice. Please. In your own time.'

# HPY 418

## An autobiography(I) from the child's seat.

HPY 418: you take the last two letters from the registration HPY 418 – so PY, look it up in the yellow book, PY = North Yorkshire. To me HPY = happy.

It's a happy van, riding in it makes you happy, it goes to happy places.
Ford Thames, a British version of the German Volkswagen van, Dad told me.

We're higher up than all the other cars. I can see everything. Panoramic.

Today we start the longest journey we've ever done. Leeds to Cornwall.

I sit on the left, Dad on the right. Everything is going to be alright, everything is in place. Yesterday Dad took the carburettor out, took the engine to pieces. He spread the Sunday Observer out on the kitchen table and took the carburettor from the cylinder head onto the paper. He said it was like the heart. On telly we saw a doctor called Christian Barnard put a new heart in a patient. I don't know anyone called Christian, anyway we're not Christians we're Catholics.

On Sunday we come back from mass and play cricket on the street. I chalked up wickets on the gate but Dad had just put the carburettor back in the engine and he parked the van right in the middle of our pitch. Dad said it was Sunday and I had to come in for dinner. That was the end of the game.

The kitchen stinks of petrol. Dad pulled out a packet of fags after dinner and I said if he lit one he'd blow us all up. He lit one but nothing happened and we're still here. So there I am in HPY on the left. The gear lever sticks out of the steering wheel. Dad pulls it down so it dislocates then slots in. Clutch in, first gear, we start moving, heading south. Cornwall. Two HPY days. Me on the left, Dad on the right.

Great.

Imagine what all the people will think when they see the Thames in Cornwall.

*1960s Devon and Cornwall tour by HPY418, 2016 by VW, with ADL*

*to whom SW 10 is dedicated with thanks.*

SW10

www.johnkinginternational.eu

**Wise Guy and other fables**, 2008

ISBN 978-0-955851902

> **Wise Guy**, 2012, is also available as an eBook at
>
> Smashwords ISBN 9781476351735

**\*Drama King**, 2010

ISBN 978-0-955851919

**Funky / Guy and other micro-fiction**, 2012

ISBN 978-0-955851964

**Micro-Waves**, 2012

ISBN 978-0-955851933

**Vienna, Love**, 2014

ISBN 978-0-955851971

**Write Coach,** 2014

ISBN 978-0-955851988

**Write Coach II** 2015

ISBN 978-0-9931306-1-8

**A and E** 2014

ISBN 978-0-955851995

**Prog** 2015

ISBN 978-0-9931306-0-1

**What's Left** 2016

ISBN 978-0-993106-2-5

**Low – Rise** 2016

ISBN 978-0-9931306-3-2

**John F King** has completed creative writing courses at


Artworks

Arvon

City Lit London

JBW London

Oxford University Department for Continuing Education

Script Yorkshire

Skyros Writers' Lab

UCLA (online), UEA / Future Learn (online)

York University Centre for Lifelong Learning


www.johnkinginternational.eu

SW10

ISBN 978-0-9931306-4-9

Author Photo

by ADL

Cornwall tour 2016

SW10

ISBN 978-0-9931306-4-9

www.ingramcontent.com/pod-product-compliance
Lightning Source LLC
Chambersburg PA
CBHW071227130626
46555CB00004B/1888